Little Sap
and
Monsieur Rodin

by Michelle Lord

illustrated by

Felicia Hoshino

Lee & Low Books Inc.
New York

For my family: Marshall, Mason, Marin, and my own little Cambodian dancer, Malia.

And for the people of Cambodia who work daily to revive their arts and culture, which were nearly erased from the world by the genocide and destruction of the Khmer Rouge in the 1970s—M.L.

To my dance teacher, Madam Michiya Hanayagi—F.H.

ACKNOWLEDGMENT
Special thanks to Toni Shapiro-Phim for reading the manuscript and sharing her expertise on the culture and dance of Cambodia.

AUTHOR SOURCES
BOOKS
Campbell, Patricia, and Sam-Ang Sam. *Silent Temples, Songful Hearts.* Danbury, CT: World Music Press, 1991.

Ghosh, Amitav. *Dancing in Cambodia, At Large in Burma.* New Delhi: Orient Longman, Ltd., 1998.

Grunfeld, Frederic. *Rodin: A Biography.* New York: Henry Holt & Co., 1987.

Guse, Ernst-Gerhard. *Auguste Rodin: Drawings and Watercolors.* Trans. John Gabriel and Michael Taylor. New York: Rizzoli, 1984.

Hale, William Harlan. *The World of Rodin.* New York: Time Life Books, 1969.

Lampert, Catherine. *Rodin: Sculpture and Drawings.* New Haven, CT: Yale University Press,1987.

Samantha-Phim, Toni. *Dance in Cambodia.* New York: Oxford University Press, 2000.

VIDEOS
Dancing Through Death: The Monkey, Magic, and Madness of Cambodia. Directed by Janet Gardner. New York: Filmmakers Library, 1999.

Khmer Studies Institute. *Khmer Court Dance.* Directed by John Bishop. Montpelier, VT: Media Generation, 1992.

WEB SITES
PBS affiliate KNPB Channel 5 Public Broadcasting Web site, "Art Beat: A. Rodin." 2003, KNPB. http://knpb.org/artbeat/rodin.

Musée Rodin official Web site. http://www.musee-rodin.fr.

Sam, Sam-Ang, "Cambodian Dance and Music in America." University of Maryland. http://research.umbc.edu/eol/cambodia/

A portion of the royalties from this book will be donated to Cambodian art and education.

Manufactured in China

Book design by David Neuhaus/NeuStudio
Book production by The Kids at Our House

The text is set in Weiss
The illustrations are rendered in ink, watercolor, acrylic, and paper collage

10 9 8 7 6 5 4 3 2 1
First Edition

Library of Congress Cataloging-in-Publication Data
Lord, Michelle.
    Little Sap and Monsieur Rodin / by Michelle Lord ; illustrated by Felicia Hoshino.— 1st ed.
        p. cm.
    Summary: In the early 1900s, Little Sap, a young girl from the rice fields of Cambodia, wins a coveted place in the royal dance troupe and learns the steps so well that she is noticed by the famous artist Auguste Rodin, who rewards her with a special prize. A foreword and an author's note give additional information about the history of Cambodia, Khmer dance, and Auguste Rodin.
    ISBN-13: 978-1-58430-248-3   ISBN-10: 1-58430-248-8
1. Cambodia—History—1863–1953—Juvenile fiction. [1. Cambodia—History—1863–1953—Fiction. 2. Dance—Fiction. 3. Rodin, Auguste, 1840–1917—Fiction.]
I. Hoshino, Felicia, ill. II. Title.
PZ7.L8777Lit 2006
[E]—dc22   2005015314

Foreword

Centered around the city of Angkor in Cambodia, the Khmer empire ruled much of Southeast Asia from the ninth through the fifteenth centuries. During this golden age, art, culture, and civic works flourished, and more than one hundred temples of brick and stone were built. Carvings on these temples showed heavenly dancers, *Apsaras.*

Due to attacks by neighboring countries, the Khmer empire began to weaken, and in 1431 the Thais conquered Angkor. The Khmer capital eventually moved to Phnom Penh, where it remains today. Throughout the following centuries, nearby countries continued to attack Cambodia until 1863, when King Norodom signed a treaty of protection with France. Soon Cambodia, along with other Southeast Asian countries, became part of French Indochina.

In 1866 King Norodom built the Royal Palace in Phnom Penh. In addition to the royal family, the palace compound housed the court dance troupe, musicians, and elephants. Young girls from throughout the kingdom began their dance training at the palace at age five or six. These girls mimicked the poses of the *Apsaras* carved on the temple walls in Angkor centuries before. The young girls danced to entertain royalty, charm the gods, and seek blessings for their people. They only left the palace to join the king on his travels across Cambodia and around the world.

One little dancer's story begins behind the walls of the Royal Palace in the early 1900s.

Khmer: pertaining to a native people of Cambodia

Little Sap stood when Princess Sisowath Soumphady tapped her baton. Peering around the room, Little Sap saw graceful girls with skin as pale and smooth as coconut milk. Her own skin had turned drab from days under the hot sun, helping Papa in the rice fields. Her feet were rough from walking barefoot. She felt like a magpie in a pen of peacocks.

Raising her heel skyward, Little Sap struggled to turn in a circle on her other foot. Princess Soumphady walked between the rows of dancers, adjusting an arm here and a knee there. Little Sap tried to hold the pose perfectly, but when the princess's firm hand pressed her shoulders back, Little Sap's heart ached with embarrassment. She wilted like a flower without sunshine, wishing she could disappear.

Girls had come from across the country to win a place in the royal dance troupe. Little Sap was lucky to have a great aunt who worked in the palace laundry, so the guards let Little Sap through just before the gates closed.

The princess chose a few girls instantly, girls with lovely moon-shaped faces and flowery names such as Bopha and Malis. Little Sap hid her dirty fingernails behind her back when Princess Soumphady came over to watch her stance and feel her muscles. Work in the fields had made Little Sap strong. The princess pointed, and helpers hustled Little Sap into the group of moon-faced girls. Little Sap had won a place in the dance troupe!

Little Sap was proud, though she knew the training would be hard. She would have to live in the Royal Palace, far away from her family and their tiny thatched house. Little Sap already missed Mama and Papa, but now she would give them a better life. Having a daughter in the royal dance troupe would raise the family's status in their village.

The first year Little Sap did not perform at all. Instead, she learned about the hundreds of movements of classical dance.

Little Sap stretched and strained. At times she wanted to quit. The training was hard and Little Sap missed her family, but she knew she must stay to make them proud.

Soon Little Sap learned to keep her face calm even when her insides jittered.

She received a silk *sampot*, pantaloons that whispered when she walked.

Little Sap learned footwork and finger symbols, breathing and balance.

She fanned out her fingers and followed the princess's slow, dipping steps across the room, making gentle shifts in her head and shoulders.

Little by little she mastered the hand motions for . . .

fruit,   flower,   and leaf!

Eventually Little Sap could touch her toes and stand on one foot.

Each day she practiced everything she had learned.

As the years passed, Sap's awkward movements began to turn into graceful poses. The poses became dances, and the dances told stories. Sap practiced to the beat of a calfskin drum: *TEP-TUP TEP-TUP-TAP*. She bent her hands like the fronds of a sugar palm curving toward the ground. Her toes curled upward. The bowl-shaped finger cymbals sang to the dancers: *CHHEPP-CHHING! CHHEPP-CHHING!*

Soon whispers from the other girls mingled with the drumbeats and chimes of the cymbals. Sap heard news of a wondrous journey. The princess would be traveling with her dancers to an exhibition in France! Sap had never before thought of leaving Cambodia. Now she was going to be dancing for important people in a faraway land across the ocean.

The day of the journey came, and Sap boarded a ship larger than any she could have imagined. The huge boat creaked and groaned under the weight of the king and his entourage, which even included a few elephants.

Sap had never felt such cold breezes. Tiny bumps raised on her arms. Her skin felt sticky. She tasted salt on her lips.

Some days the sea was smooth and the ship rocked soothingly, like the hammock of Sap's babyhood. Other days were stormy. The boat shuddered and the sea spit. Sap felt she was drifting farther and farther away from all the things she had ever known—her family and her life in the palace.

After weeks crossing uncertain seas, Sap saw France for the first time, wrapped in fog. She huddled on the deck near Princess Soumphady and the other dancers. When the ship reached port, Sap watched the crew wind thick ropes around the pilings to anchor it. The fog cleared, and Sap stared into the crowd beyond, full of feathered hats and finery. She gaped at the homes settled into the hillside. How different everything was from Cambodia!

At their first performance in Paris, Sap and the other girls danced *Robam Makaw*. The dance told the story of the sea goddess Moni, who must protect her magic crystal from the beastly Storm Spirit. Sap was so nervous she could barely breathe.

In the center of the stage, Princess Soumphady lit incense and blessed the four directions. She presented offerings to the gods before dancing. Then the dancers took the stage. Sap fluttered her fan with the younger dancers to create the sparkling scales of a sea beast. The musicians plucked strings, pounded drums, and puffed flutes.

When the dance ended, the hands of the audience blurred with clapping. A man with a furry face and tall hat gave a wild cheer. The king introduced the man as the famous French artist Auguste Rodin.

Monsieur Rodin visited the villa in the Rue Malakoff where Sap and the other dancers were staying. The artist wished to sketch the king and his dance troupe. Sap was both scared and excited to pose for this famous man. Rodin first sketched the king and the princess. Then he motioned for the dancers.

Rodin's hand dashed from side to side across his pad. Sap took her place behind Bopha, but again and again Monsieur Rodin pulled Sap to the front. Her cheeks burned and her stomach churned. The artist didn't seem to notice. He just smiled and nodded.

Sap tried to concentrate. She opened her arms and spread her fingers like a blooming lotus. The gentle *scritch scratch* of Rodin's pencil reminded Sap of the chickens scratching in the dirt back home. The thought comforted her.

After a long while, Monsieur Rodin raised his bushy eyebrows and stroked his chin. Waggling his fingers, he coaxed Sap forward once more.

"Put your foot on this," he said, pointing to the paper on his knee so that Sap understood. She tried to keep her balance as the artist carefully traced her foot.

"Now pose a little more for me!" Rodin said, twirling his hands.

Sap grew tired, but she did not stop until stars spilled into the darkened sky. She liked how the artist's eyes sparkled when she danced, as if he were seeing something magical.

After a few days, the troupe rode the train to Marseille for their next performance. Monsieur Rodin went with them. He was so eager that he brought only his pencils, his hat, and the clothes he was wearing.

The next morning Sap rubbed the sleep from her eyes and pulled on her *sampot* with shaky hands. From more than forty wonderful dancers, Monsieur Rodin had chosen only Sap and two others to pose for him.

Sap stacked bracelets on her wrists and ankles. She smoothed her shirt and walked into the garden.

Monsieur Rodin soon returned from the market with a bundle
of grocery paper on which to draw.

Sap led the dancers, asking the gods for peace and happiness
for Cambodia. She lunged and perched on the ball of her left foot.
The other girls followed. Sap drew her right foot toward her back,
which curved like the crescent moon. The music rippled over her
wrist, across her shoulders, and out through her fingertips.

For hours Rodin worked his pencil across the paper. Sap's arms
ached and her belly quaked. The other dancers rested, but Sap
danced and danced.

Finally Monsieur Rodin finished sketching and gathered his drawings. He motioned Sap over to him, and gave her a box wrapped in paper and tied with ribbon.

Sap's chest thumped like a train riding the tracks. The only present she had ever received was a scarf woven by Grandmother, given to Sap before she left home.

Sap pulled the ribbon and carefully opened the box. Inside lay a small pair of shoes like the fancy French ladies wore. She put them on and whirled in delight. The other dancers cheered and Sap felt taller than the great Eiffel Tower!

Sap hugged Rodin. As she turned away, she saw a picture of herself on the pile of drawings by his side. Her eyes widened. She looked like the heavenly dancers from the temple walls!

No longer a simple country girl, Sap had grown into a graceful dancer, carrying her people's prayers to the heavens and her family's dreams for a better life. Now she knew what the artist had seen when she danced.

Monsieur Rodin stood to go. He brought his fingers together
at his lips, then flung them into the air with a noisy kiss. Sap
nodded, palms together in the traditional way. Then Monsieur
Rodin rolled up the sketch and gently placed it in Sap's hands.

At dawn the Cambodians set sail for their homeland.

"I am deeply saddened to be leaving France," the king announced. "In this beautiful country I shall leave behind a piece of my heart."

Sap agreed. She would never forget this wondrous place or the kind man with the woolly face. She held her drawing close and her head high.

Princess Soumphady slipped her arm around Sap. She touched the drawing of Sap and smiled proudly. Sap's heart danced. Once again she felt a family's love, and home did not feel so far away.

Auguste Rodin sketching a Cambodian dancer in Marseille, 1906.

Author's Note

Not much is known about Little Sap, but I was inspired to re-create her story by blending historical facts with my memories of a trip to Cambodia. I recalled images of the beautiful countryside dotted with thatched homes on stilts and the unique beauty of Khmer dance, which dates back several centuries.

Although many details of this story are imagined, the main events are true and the dialogue is taken from actual quotes. Auguste Rodin, King Sisowath, Princess Soumphady, and Little Sap were real people whose paths crossed in France in 1906. King Sisowath took forty-two of his dancers and twelve musicians from Cambodia to perform at an exhibition of overseas French colonies. There he allowed Rodin to sketch his three favorite dancers: Sap, Soun, and Yem. The result was Rodin's famous *Danseuse Cambodgienne* sketches, which gathered acclaim when exhibited in 1907. Rodin added color washes to the sketches because the dancers' swaying bodies reminded him of flowers. Whether Rodin presented any sketches to the king or his dancers remains a mystery.

Born in 1840, Auguste Rodin overcame a meager childhood to become one of France's greatest artists. Among his best-known works are his sculptures: *The Thinker* and *The Kiss*. The inspirational effect that Sap and the other Cambodian dancers had on Rodin is clear from his own words: "When they left, everything went cold and dark. I thought that they had taken the beauty of the world away with them. . . . I followed them to Marseilles, and I could have followed them to Cairo!" In 1916, the year before his death, Rodin donated his estate containing some 7,000 drawings and 400 sculptures to the French government. Many of these great works are still enjoyed today by visitors to the Musée Rodin in Paris and other museums throughout the world.

Michelle Lord